The Wrong House

by Penny Dolan and Tomislav Zlatic

W
FRANKLIN WATTS
LONDON•SYDNEY

First published in 2011 by
Franklin Watts
338 Euston Road
London
NW1 3BH

Franklin Watts Australia
Level 17/207 Kent Street
Sydney
NSW 2000

A CIP catalogue record for this book is available
from the British Library.

ISBN 978 0 7496 9474 6 (hbk)
ISBN 978 0 7496 9480 7 (pbk)

Series Editor: Jackie Hamley
Series Advisor: Catherine Glavina
Series Designer: Peter Scoulding

Printed in China

Franklin Watts is a divison of
Hachette Children's Books,
an Hachette UK company.
www.hachette.co.uk

Cat lived in her very own
house. She knew all her
very own people.

3

She knew where
to find her food.

She knew all the good places to play ...

and sleep ...

and hide!

7

Cat knew everywhere in her own garden.

Sometimes she investigated other gardens, too.

One day, Cat went outside
and saw an open door.
She peeped in.

Then she crept in.

Then she heard feet.

Bang! The door shut.
Cat was all alone!

"Yeow, **Yeow!**"

She could not get out.

She could not find
her people.

She could not
find her food.

There was nothing
good to play with.

15

Before long, Cat heard her people calling her name.

"Yeow!" she answered,
but nobody came.

Soon it was night.
Cat could not find her
good place to sleep.
She just hid.

19

Daylight came. Cat looked up the chimney, but she could not get out that way.

Then she looked out of
the window once more.

Suddenly she heard
footsteps.

The door opened.

Whoooooosh!

Out ran Cat!

25

There was her very own

house waiting for her ...

... and her very own bowl.

Cat was so happy
to be home ...

... and her people were so happy to have her back!

Puzzle 1

a

b

c

d

e

f

Put these pictures in the correct order.
Now tell the story in your own words.
How short can you make the story?

Puzzle 2

frightened   upset

excited

delighted   thrilled

angry

Choose the words which best describe each character. Can you think of any more? Pretend to be one of the characters!

Answers

Puzzle 1

The correct order is:

1e, 2c, 3b, 4f, 5a, 6d

Puzzle 2

Cat   The correct words are frightened, upset.

The incorrect word is excited.

People   The correct words are delighted, thrilled.

The incorrect word is angry.

Look out for more Leapfrog stories:

The Little Star
ISBN 978 0 7496 3833 7

Mary and the Fairy
ISBN 978 0 7496 9142 4

Jack's Party
ISBN 978 0 7496 4389 8

Pippa and Poppa
ISBN 978 0 7496 9140 0

The Bossy Cockerel
ISBN 978 0 7496 9141 7

The Best Snowman
ISBN 978 0 7496 9143 1

Big Bad Blob
ISBN 978 0 7496 7092 4*
ISBN 978 0 7496 7796 1

Cara's Breakfast
ISBN 978 0 7496 7797 8

Croc's Tooth
ISBN 978 0 7496 7799 2

The Magic Word
ISBN 978 0 7496 7800 5

Tim's Tent
ISBN 978 0 7496 7801 2

Why Not?
ISBN 978 0 7496 7798 5

Sticky Vickie
ISBN 978 0 7496 7986 6

Handyman Doug
ISBN 978 0 7496 7987 3

Billy and the Wizard
ISBN 978 0 7496 7985 9

Sam's Spots
ISBN 978 0 7496 7984 2

Bill's Baggy Trousers
ISBN 978 0 7496 3829 0

Bill's Bouncy Shoes
ISBN 978 0 7496 7990 3

Bill's Scary Backpack
ISBN 978 0 7496 9458 6*
ISBN 978 0 7496 9468 5

Little Joe's Big Race
ISBN 978 0 7496 3832 0

Little Joe's Balloon Race
ISBN 978 0 7496 7989 7

Little Joe's Boat Race
ISBN 978 0 7496 9457 9*
ISBN 978 0 7496 9467 8

Felix on the Move
ISBN 978 0 7496 4387 4

Felix and the Kitten
ISBN 978 0 7496 7988 0

Felix Takes the Blame
ISBN 978 0 7496 9456 2*
ISBN 978 0 7496 9466 1

The Cheeky Monkey
ISBN 978 0 7496 3830 6

Cheeky Monkey on Holiday
ISBN 978 0 7496 7991 0

Cheeky Monkey's Treasure Hunt
ISBN 978 0 7496 9455 5*
ISBN 978 0 7496 9465 4

For details of all our titles go to: www.franklinwatts.co.uk

*hardback